Fern Forest's full of lovely spots.

This is the best, I'm sure.

She stops and lays her blanket down, upon the forest floor.

Then she unwraps her sandwiches.

She takes a great big bite.

Now I don't need this plastic pack.

She throws it out of sight.

The D r
Who L Floor

Russell Punter

Illustrated on

Jess shuts up her cycle store.
It's such a sunny day...
she has a picnic planned, nearby.

She munches down some crispy snacks.

The packet empties fast.

She scrunches it to make a ball...

and hurls it on the grass.

"I'll have these cookies next," she thinks.

Mmm, mint and chocolate cream.

She slings the packet overhead.

It lands **"PLOP!"** in the stream.

Jess opens up
her orange juice
and drains the
bottle dry.

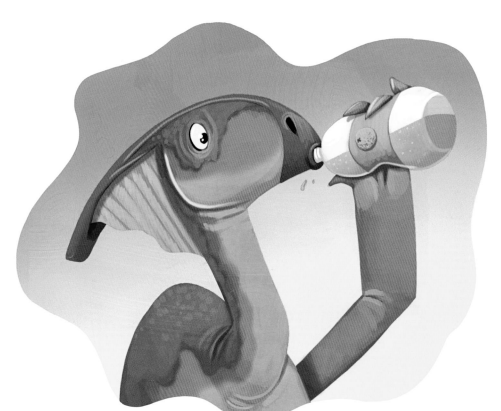

She lobs it,
WHHIZZ!
behind her back.

"Who threw that?"
comes a cry.

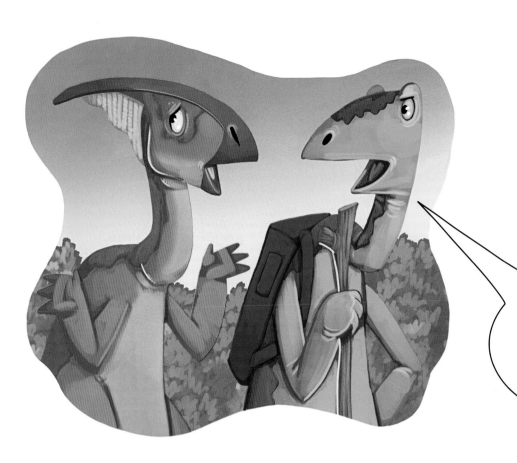

"I just threw that away," says Jess.

What, on the forest floor?

"It should go in a bin," says Sid.

But Jess just moans, "What for?"

"Well, you can pick it up," says Jess.

The others stay to clean things up.
Jess rides off on her own.

Jess hasn't gone that far when... *Eeeek!*

She hears a frightened cry.

Someone sounds unhappy...

She goes to find out why.

Jess finds a
baby platypus.
Its foot is stuck.

How sad!

She takes the bottle
off its leg.

Now Jess is
feeling bad.

Jess rides back to her cycle store.
She starts work on her plan.

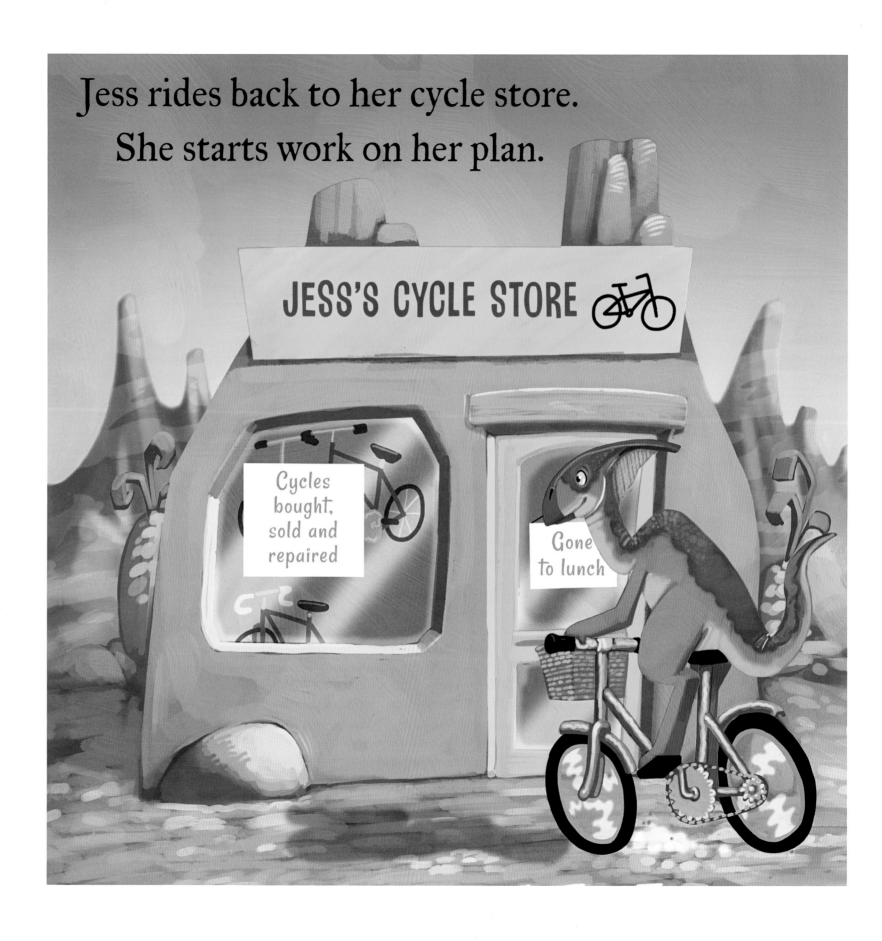

She **BANGS**...

and **CLANGS**...

and **SCREWS**...

and **GLUES**...

as quickly as she can.

She heads back to the forest.

Hey, what's Jess riding now?

"You ride it over litter,
which sticks on spikes
that spin.

Next, it's scooped
from off the spikes...

...and ends up in the bin."

"What a great idea," says Sid.

"So clever too!" Ross cries.

"We're glad you've changed your ways," says Sue.

RECYCLING BIKE

It's such a nice surprise!

So Jess heads off, upon her bike,
and makes the forest clean.

Soon every piece of litter's gone.
All thanks to her machine.

The visitors are all impressed.

"You've worked so hard," they say.

"We'll do our best to keep things clean and throw all our mess away!"

Edited by Lesley Sims

Digital manipulation by Nick Wakeford